Snow White

Fairy Tale Treasury

Adapted by
Jane Jerrard

Illustrations by
Burgandy Nilles

Publications International, Ltd.

Long ago, a princess was born. The little princess, called Snow White, grew more beautiful every year. Her stepmother, the Queen, was also very beautiful and so proud that she had a magical mirror made. Every day she would ask the mirror,

"Mirror, mirror on the wall,
Who is fairest of us all?"

The mirror would answer that the Queen was fairest in the land.

But one day when the Queen asked the mirror who was the fairest in the land, the mirror replied,

"You, my Queen, may lovely be,
But Snow White's fairer still than thee."

The Queen was very angry. She called a woodsman and told him to kill Snow White. The man couldn't bring himself to kill the girl, so he led her into the woods and left her.

Snow White was frightened by the noises in the woods. She began to run. She ran as fast and as far as she could, until she saw a little cottage with a red roof. When no one answered her knock, Snow White went inside.

There she found a little table set with seven plates, and seven little beds all lined up. The tired princess threw herself down on the seventh bed and fell fast asleep.

Now, seven dwarfs shared that little cottage, and they soon came back from mining gold all day. How surprised they were to find Snow White asleep in their home!

When Snow White awoke, they asked her how she had found her way to their cottage. When they heard Snow White's story, they asked her to stay. She took care of the cottage, and they gave her food, shelter, and friendship in return.

One day back at the castle, the evil Queen asked her mirror who was the fairest, and the mirror told her that Snow White still lived.

Disguising herself as an old woman, she found her way to the little cottage. "Belts for sale!" she called.

Snow White was eager to try on one of the lovely belts. The Queen pulled the belt so tight around the girl's waist that she fell as if dead.

The dwarfs returned to find Snow White lying on the floor. They saw that the girl's belt was too tight and cut it off. She awoke and told them what had happened. The dwarfs realized that this was the work of the Queen, and they warned Snow White to be very careful.

When the evil Queen learned from her mirror that Snow White was still the fairest, she shook with rage. The Queen vowed that Snow White must die.

The evil Queen set out in a new disguise and offered to sell Snow White a lovely comb. Snow White put the comb in her hair and fell where she stood, for the comb was poisoned. The dwarfs returned and saw the deadly comb at once. They quickly took it from Snow White's hair before it killed her.

When the Queen learned that the girl still lived, she used all her magic to make a poisoned apple.

Then she dressed herself as a poor woman and went once more to see Snow White. When she offered the girl the apple, Snow White bit into it and instantly fell as if dead.

When the Queen returned to the castle, her mirror told her at last, "Queen, thou art fairest of all!"

The dwarfs could not save Snow White. They laid her in a glass case so they could watch over her.

One day, a Prince came upon the lovely girl lying in the glass case. Thinking she must be under an evil spell, he opened the case. When the Prince lifted Snow White, the apple fell from her lips and she awoke.

The dwarfs were delighted to see Snow White alive and agreed that she should marry the Prince. As for the Queen, her hatred made her so ugly that she shattered her magic mirror.